INVESTIGATING MYSTERIOUS PLACES

ROSWELL

ALIEN CAPITAL OF THE WORLD

by Allan Morey

CAPSTONE PRESS
a capstone imprint

Published by Capstone Press, an imprint of Capstone
1710 Roe Crest Drive, North Mankato, Minnesota 56003
capstonepub.com

Copyright © 2025 by Capstone. All rights reserved. No part of this publication may be reproduced in whole or in part, or stored in a retrieval system, or transmitted in any form or by any means, electronic, mechanical, photocopying, recording, or otherwise, without written permission of the publisher.

Library of Congress Cataloging-in-Publication Data is available on the Library of Congress website.

ISBN: 9781669093572 (hardcover)
ISBN: 9781669093527 (paperback)
ISBN: 9781669093534 (ebook PDF)

Summary: Take a trip to Roswell, New Mexico, where a mysterious UFO crash sparked decades of stories about aliens. What really happened in the so-called Alien Capital of the World, and are there secrets still waiting to be uncovered?

Editorial Credits
Editor: Donald Lemke; Designer: Tracy Davies; Media Researcher: Svetlana Zhurkin; Production Specialist: Katy LaVigne

Image Credits
Alamy: Charles Walker Collection, 6; Courtesy, Fort Worth Star-Telegram Photograph Collection, Special Collections, The University of Texas at Arlington Library, Arlington, Texas: 21, 25, 26; Dreamstime: Mark Wilson, 11, Palms, 28; Getty Images: David Zaitz, 7, DigitalStorm, 19, Max2611, 13, Science Photo Library/KTSDesign, 5, Science Photo Library/Victor Habbick Visions, 23, Siqui Sanchez, 9, UIG/Mark Stevenson, cover, back cover, 1; Shutterstock: Aliaksei Hintau (smoke background), 2 and throughout, Andrei Tudoran, 12, ehrlif, 18, Fer Gregory, 17, Kit Leong, 10, PeopleImages-Yuri A, 29, Vector Tradition (alien icon), cover and throughout; SuperStock: Image Asset Management/World History Archive, 15; U.S. Air Force: 27

Any additional websites and resources referenced in this book are not maintained, authorized, or sponsored by Capstone. All product and company names are trademarks™ or registered® trademarks of their respective holders.

TABLE OF CONTENTS

Chapter One
UFOs 4

Chapter Two
ROSWELL 8

Chapter Three
THE CRASH 14

Chapter Four
THE TRUTH? 20

GLOSSARY 30
READ MORE 31
INTERNET SITES 31
INDEX 32
ABOUT THE AUTHOR 32

Chapter One

UFOs

What is a UFO? It is an Unidentified Flying Object. These flying objects, or **phenomena**, cannot be explained.

Many people think UFOs are alien spacecraft. They imagine flying saucers. They picture **extraterrestrials** from other worlds.

For hundreds of years, people have seen unusual flashing lights in the sky. They have spotted strange flying crafts. Many of these sightings could not be explained. Some sightings led to wild stories of alien visitors.

A UFO flying over the Alps in 1952

Sign directing to the supposed UFO crash site in Roswell, New Mexico

One of the most well-known stories happened in 1947. It took place in Roswell, New Mexico. This story helped spark a UFO craze!

FACT

In 1947, Pilot Kenneth Arnold came up with the term "flying saucer." He described some unknown craft he saw as looking like plates, or saucers.

Chapter Two

ROSWELL

Roswell, New Mexico, is a small city of about 46,000 people. It lies about 200 miles (320 kilometers) southeast of Albuquerque, the state's largest city.

Walker Air Force Base sits just outside of the town. The base was built in 1941. It was first used as a training school for pilots.

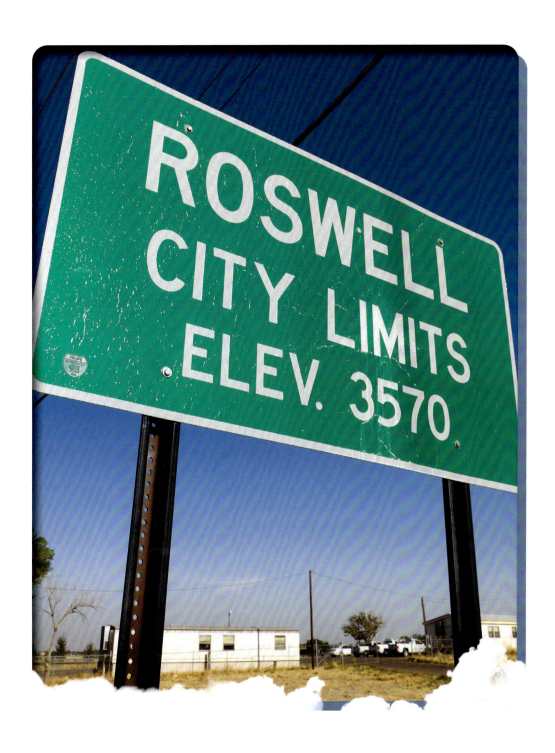

The International UFO Museum and Research Center in Roswell

Roswell seems to be a small, normal American city—except for one thing. UFOs! In fact, the International UFO Museum and Research Center is located in Roswell.

The city also holds a yearly UFO Festival. There are many UFO statues and attractions throughout the city as well.

People in alien costumes take part in Roswell's UFO Festival.

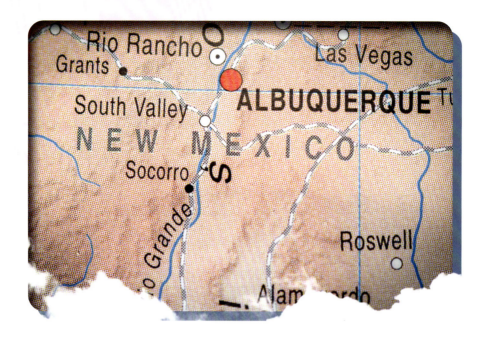

But why are people in Roswell so interested in aliens?

It all started back in 1947. Rancher Mac Brazel found something strange on his farm. Many people thought this something **proved** that UFOs were real.

FACT

In 1947, people around the world reported more than 300 UFO sightings.

Chapter Three

THE CRASH

Things started getting strange near Roswell on June 14, 1947. A storm blew through the area. Afterward, Brazel found **debris** on his farm. To many, the materials he found looked to be from another world!

A local newspaper article about the Roswell UFO incident from July 8, 1947

Then, on the night of July 2, strange lights appeared whizzing overhead. People in the city reported hearing odd swishing sounds.

On July 7, Brazel visited the town's sheriff. In the back of his pickup truck, he had some of the debris. When officials from the military base heard about it, they came to haul the debris away.

That was not the end of the strange stories. Workers near Socorro, New Mexico, claimed to have found a crashed disc-shaped craft.

Nearby, they said, lay the body of a dead alien. It had large eyes and gray skin.

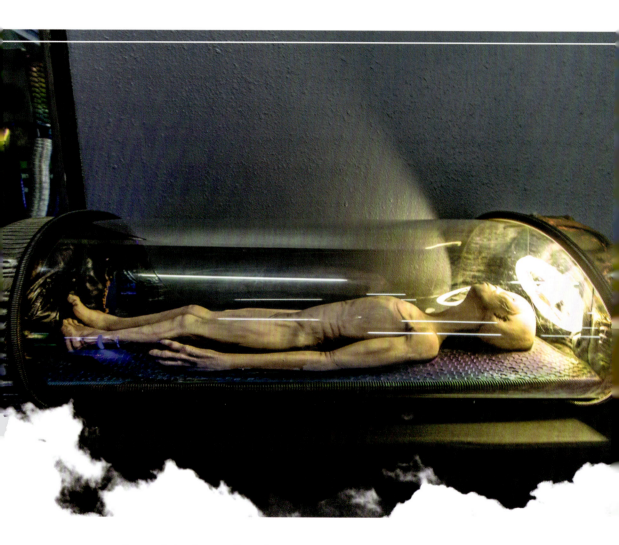

A model of an alien in a protective tube is displayed at Roswell's UFO Museum.

Many UFO stories suggest the government kept the research secret.

Again, military officials swooped in and took everything away. The debris was flown to an air base in Fort Worth, Texas, to be tested.

FACT

From 1947 to 1969, Project Blue Book was a military mission to investigate reported UFO sightings.

Chapter Four

THE TRUTH?

On July 8, 1947, military officials said that a flying saucer had been found near Roswell. But hours later, newspapers reported that the debris actually came from a weather balloon.

Which was true?

An officer holds pieces of the supposed UFO identified as remains of a military research balloon.

The **conflicting** reports made people **suspicious**. Was this all a military cover-up? Were officials hiding something?

Perhaps military officials were trying to hide the truth. But not proof of UFOs. Rather, a secret military project.

Project Mogul was a top-secret spy project. It involved high-flying balloons that carried microphones to search for far-off sounds.

Project Mogul's main purpose was to detect whether the Soviet Union was testing nuclear weapons. At that time, only the United States had nuclear bombs.

Airmen attaching a radar device to a weather balloon at Fort Worth Air Base on July 11, 1947

An airman holds on to a cable connected to a weather balloon carrying a radar device.

The balloons were different than regular weather balloons. They were made of **reflective** foil. Parts of the balloons were odd shapes and connected by a long cable. To the average person, they may have looked alien.

And what of the alien body that was found? A 1997 military report stated that it was a test dummy from a parachute experiment.

A dummy with a parachute (left) is getting ready for launch at a test site in New Mexico, 1953.

An alien gift shop in Roswell, New Mexico

Reports from the military easily explained away the idea aliens from outer space were involved in the Roswell **Incident**. But not everyone believes those reports. Just walk around Roswell.

There are many monuments to space aliens. They are proof that a lot of people still believe in UFOs. The mysteries of what happened in Roswell have not all been answered.

Belief that aliens and UFOs may be real continues to capture people's imagination.

Glossary

conflicting (kon-FLIK-ting)—when two things do not agree or are opposite

debris (duh-BREE)—pieces of stuff left over after something breaks apart

extraterrestrial (eks-truh-tuh-RES-tree-uhl)—anything that comes from outside Earth, especially alien life-forms

incident (IN-sih-dent)—an event or something that happens, typically important or unusual

phenomena (fuh-NOM-uh-nah)—things that are unusual or hard to explain

prove (PROOV)—to show the truth by using evidence

reflective (re-FLEK-tiv)—something that bounces light back, like a mirror or shiny surface

suspicious (suh-SPIH-shus)—feeling doubt or mistrust about something, thinking it might not be right or true

Read More

Bolte, Mari. *Area 51 and Other Top Secret Science.* Ann Arbor, Mich.: Cherry Lake Publishing Group, 2023.

Cruz, Jose. *Area 51, Lizard People, and More Conspiracy Theories about the Unexplained.* North Mankato, MN.: Capstone Press, 2025.

Deniston, Natalie. *Area 51.* Minneapolis: Jump!, Inc., 2025.

Internet Sites

History.com: Roswell
history.com/topics/paranormal/roswell

Kiddle: Roswell Incident Facts for Kids
kids.kiddle.co/Roswell_incident

Roswell, New Mexico: Our History
roswell-nm.gov/654/Our-History

Index

Albuquerque, New Mexico, 8
aliens, 4, 6, 18, 27, 28
Arnold, Kenneth, 7

Brazel, Mac, 12, 14, 16

flying saucers, 4, 7, 20
Fort Worth, Texas, 19, 25

International UFO Museum and Research Center, 10

military, 16, 19, 20, 21, 22, 25, 27, 28

Project Mogul, 24

Roswell, New Mexico, 7, 8, 28, location of, 8

Socorro, New Mexico, 16
spying, 24

UFO Festival, 11
UFOs, 4, 6, 7, 10, 11, 12, 15, 19, 21

Walker Air Force Base, 8
weather balloon, 20, 25, 26

About the Author

Some of Allan Morey's favorite childhood memories are from the time he spent on a farm in Wisconsin. Every day he saw cows, chickens, and sheep. He even had a pet pig named Pete. He developed a great appreciation of animals, big and small. Allan currently lives in St. Paul with his family and dogs, Stitch and Enzo, who keep him company while he writes.